Murdoch Mole
Digs For Gold

Murdoch Mole
Digs For Gold

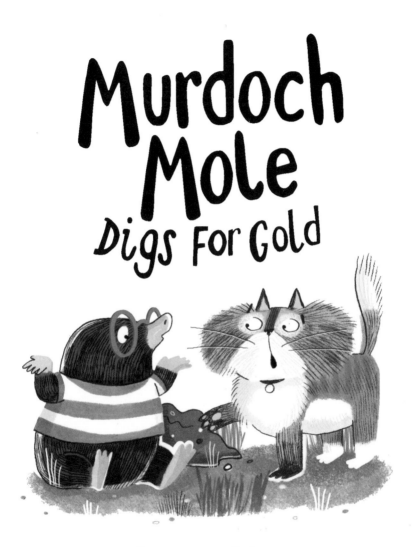

Georgie Adams
Illustrated by Pippa Curnick

Orion
Children's Books

ORION CHILDREN'S BOOKS

First published in Great Britain in 2016
by Hodder and Stoughton

1 3 5 7 9 10 8 6 4 2

Text © Georgie Adams 2016
Illustrations © Pippa Curnick 2016

The moral rights of the author and illustrator have been asserted.

A CIP catalogue record for this book
is available from the British Library.

ISBN 978 1 4440 1160 9

Printed and bound in China

The paper and board used in this book are from well-managed forests
and other responsible sources.

Orion Children's Books
An imprint of
Hachette Children's Group
Part of Hodder and Stoughton

Carmelite House
50 Victoria Embankment
London EC4Y 0DZ

An Hachette UK Company
www.hachette.co.uk

www.hachettechildrens.co.uk

For Esme Wren Errington with love – G.A.

*To the Burbidges, whose sheep and ducks
were my inspiration! – P.C.*

Chapter One

Murdoch Mole loves to dig!
His molehills pop up all
over Farmer Becky's farm.

In winter Murdoch's molehills
make wonderful slides.

In spring they are fun to
jump over!

"You are clever!" says Bert.
"Thank you," says Murdoch.
Farmer Becky does not agree.

"I wish Murdoch would do something useful," she says. "His molehills make such a mess!"

One morning, Bert and
Becky were in the cornfield.
"I see Murdoch has been
here," says Becky.

"His molehills are spoiling my corn! There will be no money to feed my animals. That mole has to go!"

Oh dear, thinks Bert.
I must warn Murdoch!

Bert finds Murdoch in the
farmyard.

"You're in big trouble,"
says Bert.

"Me?" says Murdoch.
"Why?"

"Your molehills are spoiling
the corn," says Bert.
"If there isn't any corn to
sell, Becky can't buy food
for her animals."

"No food?" grunts Pig.

"No hay? No way!"
shouts Horse.

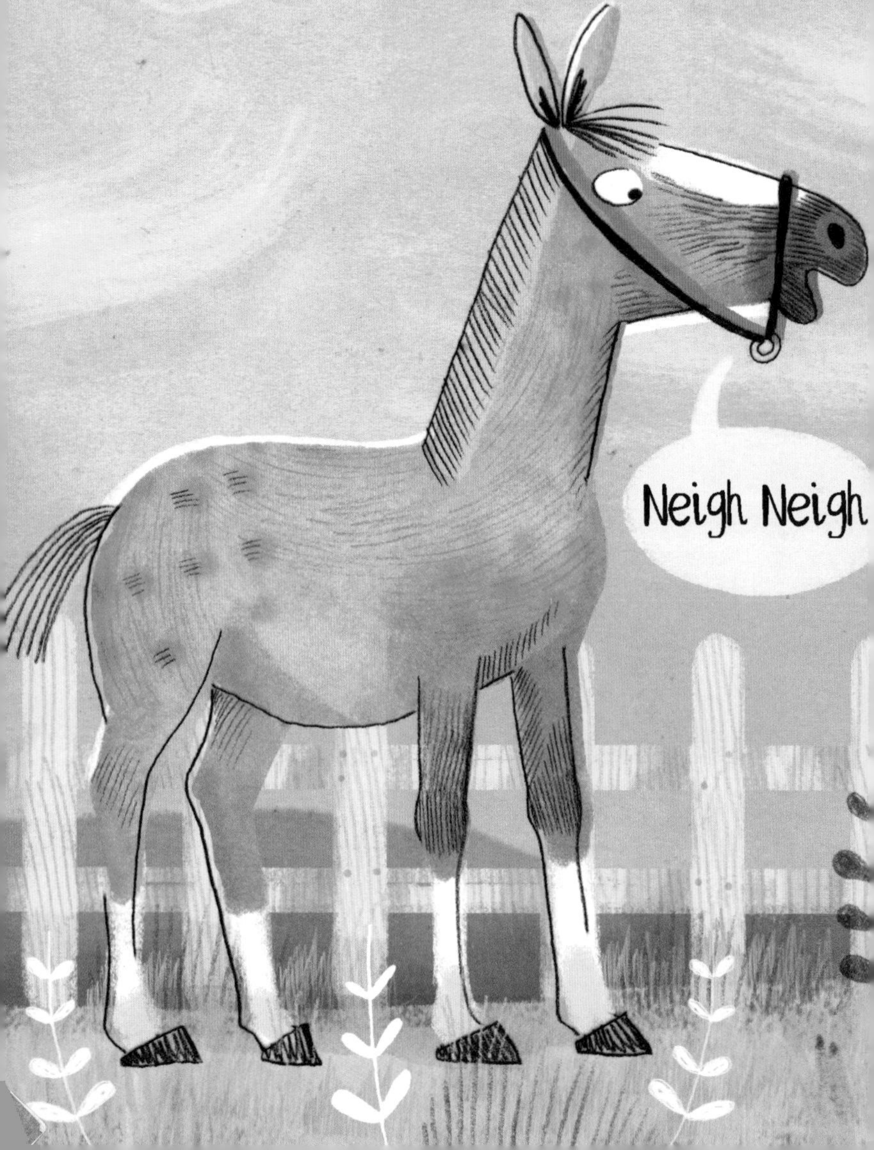

"That won't dooooooo!"
says Cow.

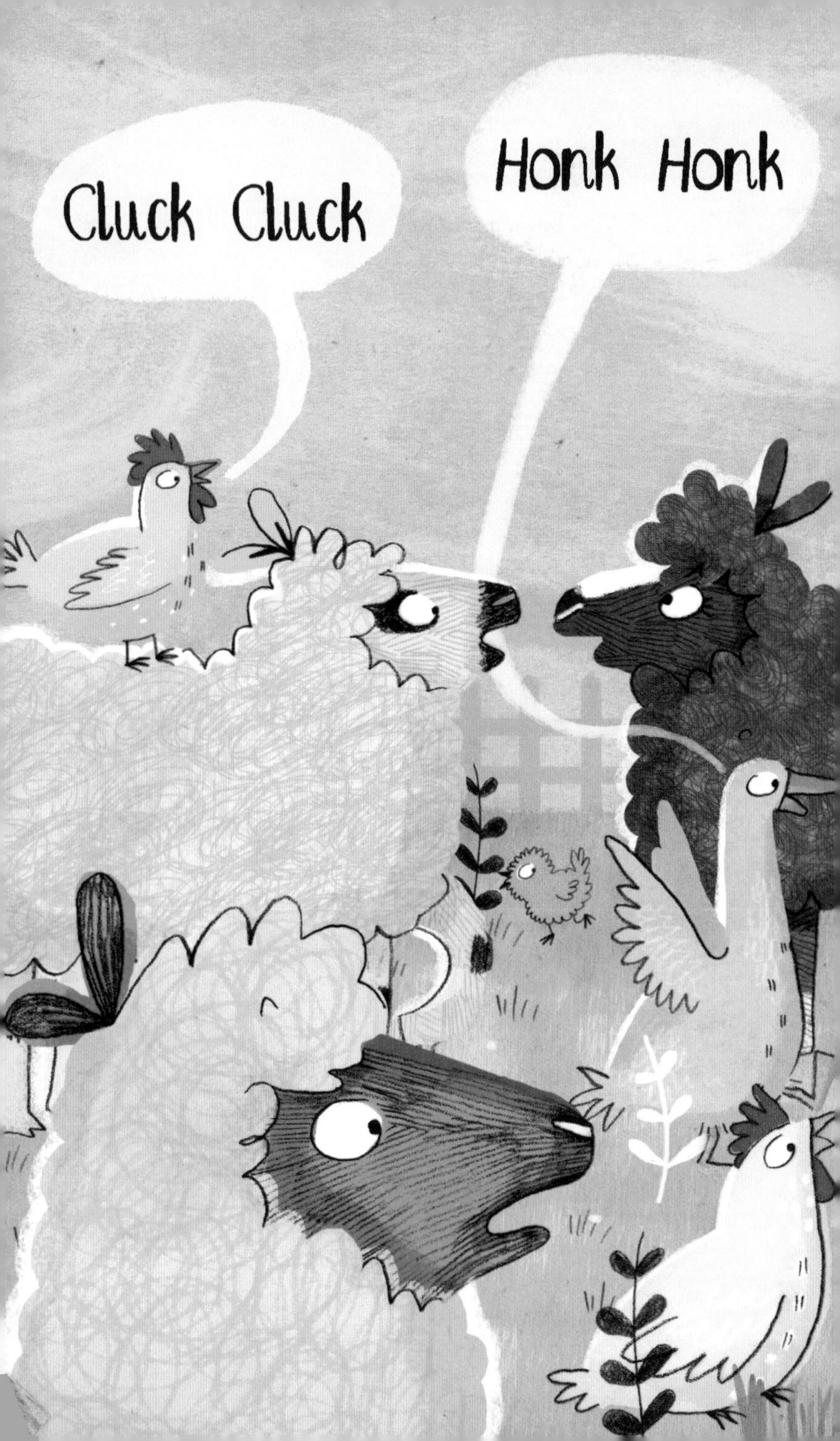
Cluck Cluck
Honk Honk

Murdoch is upset.

"Oh dear," he says.

"But I have to eat too.

That cornfield is full of worms!"

"Maybe you could try
somewhere else?" says Bert.
"All right," says Murdoch.
"I will."

So Murdoch digs a new tunnel.

along the carrots

marrows

and ends up in the marrows.

cabbages

carrots

It goes under the cabbages,

Murdoch is pleased with his
work. He finds a nice, fat
worm too.

"Perfect!" says Murdoch as
he settles down for a nap.
Suddenly, he hears a shout.

"My vegetables!" cries Becky. "Just wait till I catch you, Murdoch Mole!"

Murdoch hurries away as
fast as his little legs can go.
"I wish I could find
somewhere good to dig."
he says.

Carrots

Soon it is summer, but there
aren't enough sunny days to
ripen the corn.

It pours with rain, and
Becky's crop is ruined.

By autumn, Becky doesn't
have any money left.
"I will have to sell the
farm," Becky tells Bert
sadly, one windy day.

Bert wishes he could help.
He gives the bad news to
the animals.

The pigs, the horses, the cows, the sheep, the geese, the ducks and the hens are very upset.

They all love the farm.
They love Farmer Becky!

Then Bert goes to find
Murdoch. In the orchard,
he spots a molehill by an
old apple tree.

Bert hurries over.
The wind blows hard.
Whoooo-Whoooooo!

The old tree sways and apples fall to the ground. One hits poor Bert on the nose. Bonk!
"Ouch!" says Bert.

It lands on top of the
molehill with a bump!
"Hey! What's going on?"
says Murdoch.

Bert points to the apple.
Then he sees something else.
"What's that?" says Bert.

"Rubbish!" says Murdoch.
"It's blocking my tunnel."

Bert tells Murdoch about Becky's troubles.

"I want to help," says Murdoch. "But I'm only a mole. What can I do?"

Just then, a strong gust of wind blows the tree down. The old apple tree falls with
a CRACK!

and a CRASH!

"Goodness!" says Murdoch.
Becky comes running into
the orchard to see what has
happened.

"Uh-oh!" says Bert.

"What a shame!" cries Becky. "First, the rain ruins my corn. Now, the wind has blown down my apple tree. It's the last straw!"

Becky gives the molehill a
kick. Suddenly something
shiny catches her eye.

Becky picks it up and brushes away the dirt. "A bracelet!" she cries.
"A beautiful gold bracelet."

And there is more. . .
gold coins,

a necklace,

a brooch,

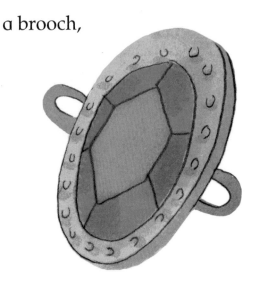

a piece of pottery.

"Ooo!" says Becky. "These look very old. Just think. There's treasure right under our feet!"

"Treasure?" says Murdoch.
"I call it rubbish! There's
lots more under the tree."

"It's treasure!" says Bert.
"You're good at digging,
Murdoch. Maybe you could
dig it up?"

"Leave this to me!"
says Murdoch.

"Murdoch!" says Becky. But this time she doesn't sound cross. Becky can't believe how much more treasure Murdoch has found.

"Thank you very much,
Murdoch Mole!" says Becky.
"You've done something
really useful. I can sell the
treasure and keep my farm."

Becky gives Murdoch his
very own place in the orchard,
which was full of worms.
"Thank you," says Murdoch
happily. "At last, I have
somewhere good to dig."

"Well done," says Bert.
"You've saved the day.
Three cheers for Murdoch Mole!"
Hooray! Hooray! Hooray!

What are you going to read next?

Don't miss
magic and adventure in the
Three Little stories.

football fun
in **Albert and the
Garden of Doom**,

or Timothy
making a special
mud pie in
Chocolate Porridge.